I0538341

This Book Belongs To:

_____

Solstice

of

Sorrow

A tale told in two parts.

Written By Alexis Elizabeth Lynch
Illustrated By Kevin Edwards

Library of Congress Control Number: 2017918270
AEL Library & Archives (AELLA), London OH

Print Edition ISBN: 978-0692986769
Digital Edition ASIN: B0785WZV1P

First Edition printed December 2017.
Printed and bound in the United States of America.

Cover & Illustrations © Kevin Edwards
Map & Layout: © Thomas S Nicol

The typeface used: ©Laandbrau by Intellecta Design, and
Times New Roman, and High Tower Text.

Fiction/Gothic

Dedicated to:

My incredible Mother Elizabeth Lynch.
&
My best friend and Cousin Adam Edwards.

They have been both my sounding boards and brainstorming companions; offering valuable feedback and insight into my work while remaining free of personal judgment. It is because of them that I have become the writer I am today. I love them both dearly.

And to Michael McHenry;
*It happened suddenly, and far too soon.
Loosing you still hurts.*

"He who fights with monsters should be careful lest he thereby become a monster. And if thou gaze long into an abyss, the abyss will also gaze into thee. The tormentor becomes the tormented. People become what they love and hate because their mind focuses on it."

-Friedrich Wilhelm Nietzsche

Part 1

Solstice

of

Sorrow

Alexis Elizabeth Lynch

Chapter 1

The Village

Alexis Elizabeth Lynch

Solstice of Sorrow

There lay a village far to the north, located just south of a sheer mountain ridge, and the coniferous forest that lay at its feet. The dwelling is surrounded by no wall, and the only road from town is a trade route that leads southward. The seasons change, crops are sown and harvested, and snow is on the land for most of the year. Even in the warm times of the cycle, rain falls in snows place, and the mists from the mountains crying and trees breathing, lay over the land in a thick fog. The roots of the people go back to the very first who dwelled here; the Ancients. Having adapted well for hundreds of years since they do not lack for sustenance; hunting and gathering by day in the vast forest, tending crops and livestock, and fishing from the river that flows through the town; it's origin a many-fingered mountain-fed lake deep in the forest to the north.

Though their ancestors dwelled inside the great forest itself, the people no longer do. Once the moon rises, no one leaves the village, nor dares to enter the forest. Farmers and animals alike turning in after a long day working in the sun. The called-for children and dogs running like water through the streets and into their houses. Hunters search for prey among the trees during the hours when the sun is the highest in the sky. All work, burials, and traveling are done by the light of day. Even if the beasts come in the night, those who are taken are not searched for until the sun rises. To do otherwise is a sure death.

The people are quite changed from their ancestors; a people of magic and knowledge, survival, and herbalism. Most are now farmers, blacksmiths, hunters, and midwives. Since the time of the first times, the wisdom of the ancients has been lost, and magic has been dead in the land. Only wise women and healers and those spending years bent over their books and papers have some small art or knowledge of the craft. Even then, they do not know the old magic. Other than the spoken word tales passed from year to year, there are no remaining texts or records of those ancient peoples, nor the times of when the beasts roamed the land. It is said the writings were destroyed in the cataclysm which took them all; the Curse. Though the people's complacency of hundreds of years could as easily ridicule and discredit those old texts, even if they did exist.

Just beyond the fields and orchards, inside the tree line of the forest, lay remnants that are the only surviving relics of the ancestors who first tamed the land and who were the first to encounter the beasts. It is said a curse befell them, though those circumstances are now long shrouded in mystery. It is known that the ancestors had magic; the sort studied and practiced and woven into every element of their world. It is said they vanquished the beasts with their magic, though their ultimate destruction tells otherwise. All that remains; their sacred burial grounds, which have been used every generation since to house the dead. It is the most sacred place, a place that has been touched by magic, where the dirt holds the bones of a great people of knowledge and power. And a curse. The burial ground is circular in nature, graves surrounded by a vast stone wall, long since covered with a layer of thick moss and vines of ivy. There has always been room inside the circular walls to lay more to rest, no matter how many years pass or how many are buried. When winter is upon them and snow blankets the land, during the time of the Solstice-red ferns push up from under the white snow to grow atop each burial place. No one plants them and yet they still grow. The trees here are ancient, towering and mighty, their roots crawling across the mossy boulder-strewn forest floor. Despite this, the burial grounds lay smooth, untouched by tree roots or rock alike-the wall itself seemingly protective.

The burials are continued in the traditional way; dug into the ground, and afterward covered entirely with piles of stones. A large rock serves as the headpiece; epitaphs carved in the old runic language, bearing the true name of the deceased. The true name of which could only be known or spoken aloud by others once the person had passed on. Though upon death, their common face-name could not be spoken aloud any longer-for the dead cannot rest when being called for by name by those left behind. The worst kind of death was to be taken by the beasts. A body and soul not able to be cleansed can never find peace; to spend forever and an eternity wandering among the snow and trees. A soul must be allowed to find its way to the eternity from which all things come, back to the fabric from which all things are made. For the people, death is a part of life, and without one there couldn't be the other. All creatures, beings, and elements of nature have an end in their own time. Even the stars die, and from that are born worlds of new. And so are the beliefs of the people, which were passed down from those who came before them.

Alexis Elizabeth Lynch

Chapter 2

The Curse

Alexis Elizabeth Lynch

Solstice of Sorrow

Tales of the beasts and their curse have been passed down through each generation. Every child in town, few as there may be, can tell the stories of the beasts, and what they bring with them upon the winds of the night. Old women, grandmothers, wet nurses, and elders, rock back and forth, huddled in chairs next to roaring fire-sides. Small children set upon their laps and curl up wide-eyed around their feet. They lean close in anticipation of each whisper from the old crone's toothless mouth, small sweaty-palmed hands grasping desperately to the hem of her gown and robes. *"You must never speak the name of those dead the beasts have taken! For they know each one they have consumed, and they can hear even a whisper in the dark. The beasts will run as Hessians ride, to the door of the one who spoke it. They will find you and no one else will ever again! Such is their dire nature. They call forth the rain, the trembling thunder, and even your horrible nightmares. Their howls can ensnare a man into their waiting jaws, and beware to those they smell of the nights of a full moon. For there is no force that can stop them, and even your cries to the Gods go unheard."*

In olden times, it was believed the beasts themselves were Gods of a sort; bringing forth the storms, conjuring the fog, their howls chasing the sun past the horizon and revealing the night. It was thought that the moon was the very eye of the beasts; all seeing, all knowing, a beacon of both light in the dark as well as a dismal reminder of no escape. One cannot hide from the moon. And so it has been since the time these tales were begun. But genera-tions have born and died, hundreds of years passed, but the rain still falls, and the moon still rises, without any sign of the beasts' existence. The seasons change and life here continues, and the beasts themselves became nothing more than monsters of myth and specters of superstition.

Traveling merchants to the Northern Territory are few and far between, and even they arrive before dark, hoods up and shoulders hunched and startled by every whiney of a horse or gust of wind. Some of the tales told are false; changed and imagined over time, history nearly forgotten, and a once-prominent daily retribution forged into fables. Little do they know, most of the time legends are based on truths.

Much can be forgotten as the years pass, seasons wax and wane and time carries on. It is hard after the complacency of hundreds of years to come to terms with the fact of a town's traditions and tales and ceremonies, to have been founded on a malevolent truth. Fires kept burning night after night, year after year, for the desperate survival of a people, rather than reasons of cultural preservation of a town. They still pray to the gods of their ancestors. The Gods of plants and water and stone. The Gods of the turning seasons and man's labor, and the sun and moon. The midwife God, the warrior God, the Gods of creatures and weather and fire. The Gods of knowledge and even the Gods of death-those who take the soul to its final resting place. Every man's home and heart is his temple. Every God granted their strength to exist, buy the strength of the people's belief in them. Though, their lessons are not entirely taken to heart. This is the way of the people, as it has been since the seasons first started changing in the beginning.

Chapter 3

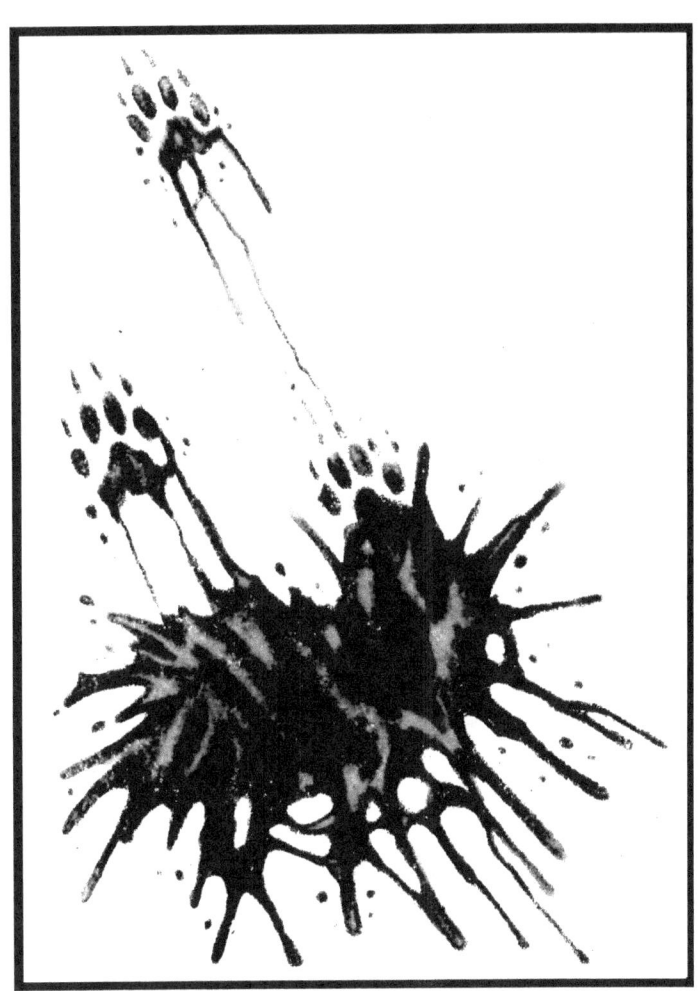

The Beast

Alexis Elizabeth Lynch

Solstice of Sorrow

There is no physical evidence that the beasts roam the land once again, other than the blood left pooling where living men once stood. It is said the beasts themselves are ghosts and spirits. They are like shadows, paws treading softly across the ground, moving as mist between the houses. Their tracks seemed to dissolve into the ground only minutes after sunrise, erasing all trace of where they once stalked. The prints, scarcely left in only the muddiest of conditions, and atop of snow, are rarely seen by the eyes of man. It was said by one of the only men ever to lay eyes on the tracks, that it was so large that he could place his spread hand in the center of the track, and his fingers do not come close to the edges of the pad. Each toe the size of his closed fist. The slices pressed into the ground from the claws, as if a man had driven his knife into the earth with a curse against the land. It is also said that they are flesh and blood, somewhat wolf-like in nature but nothing from nature itself. A wolf is sheer power; a prey in fear only making the chase more empowering for them. Their hunts-ruthless and not always quick. The brutality of being eaten alive enough to make anyone wary. But wolves can be shot; they can be killed. Unlike the beasts who seemed to be such an unstoppable force, like the wind or the tides.

More lately than before, rain comes with the moon. Wet wood can hardly be lit; even the oil-drenched pine logs smoke out in the storms. The villagers make the sign of the Gods over themselves and swear that they are cursed. The fires must always be lit before the sun sinks entirely, swallowed by the horizon. The fires must be lit before the moon rises. Their superstitions run deep. Then everything changed and suddenly; the stories of their ancestors were manifesting all around them. Life now a nightmare spilled over into waking hours. So they took up arms and barred the doors and windows. Blowing out the candles and lamps and putting the fires to sleep in the hearths, they waited, in absolute darkness, for the screams, a sound, a sign. Breathing softly and scarcely moving till sunrise. Dark charcoal smoke reeking of oil and flame rises like steam over the rooftops, twisting and curling into ill omens of destruction. The moonlight illuminates fields of cornstalks plowed under, deserted streets, restless livestock and a village holding its breath.

Since the beasts have returned, a man's faith in his Gods has dwindled. So much death, bloodshed, and sleepless nights where prayers whispered behind locked doors and cried pleadingly out into the night go unheard. A cry of desperation now like the squalling of a child, alone in all the world with its cruelty. Some say the Gods have abandoned them, and others that they were never there in the first place. Some yet say the village and the people are under the same curse as their ancestors. That it is all retribution.

Let us be frank about this; there is no reason for the villagers to hide. The beasts know where every living being is. They can smell the sweat and fear of the small children, huddled and weeping silently under the floorboards of the houses, and in the passages of the cellars. They can hear the high-frequency whines of the anxious dogs laying guard by the doors; a sound too quiet for human ears. The smell of warm blood and flesh is so pungent in their noses they can taste it in their joules. Every human in the village reeks of fear; their pheromones a database of information to the snout; males, females, young, elderly, pregnant, pubescent, menstruating, males no longer producing seed, babies fresh from the womb, those close to drawing their last breaths. The darkness, the silence, the locks and dogs and guns and lookouts, the hiding, all done to comfort the madness of anticipation, to guard their minds against complete breakdown from fear. How could one bare the weight of knowing there is no escape?

Snow falls lightly, dusting the dark pines with soft glittery white, and settling silently onto the fur of the beasts; slicked black as oil, matted down with cakes of dried blood. The snowflakes stand out violently against the dark fur until suddenly melting into nothing; their very structure dissolving, consumed without mercy from the heat of the beasts' running bodies. They move through the trees smooth and sharp like sharks through the water. Pads pressing silently into the snow-covered ground, and then; the tracks are gone too as if only the wind ran through the trees.

Alexis Elizabeth Lynch

Chapter 4

The Attacks

Alexis Elizabeth Lynch

Sometimes there is no warning. No clue of what happens beyond the buildings. Sometimes there is not a noise to break the silence the entire night, the only sign that it's over, being the sun rising over the treetops. The morning comes to dirt in the fields darkened with blood splatters and gushing trails leading into the forest. To-night, was not a night like that; the worst of silent nights, hours spent in the turmoil of waiting. A heavy darkness lay over everything, dense and consuming as a black hole, pressing on the chests of those alive like a great stone, sucking the very breath from their lungs and the reflection of light from the eyes. Even the pale light of the full moon seems dimmed, the shadows more profound and inescap-able than before.

Just beyond the village, along the tree line of the forest, the men keep watch. Up all night with the moon, waiting anxiously for death to come. A man is silhouetted by the moonlight, walking in a harvested cornfield. His hair more grey than not, a bolt-action rifle tucked under his arm, a large hunting knife in a leather sheath on his belt. He paces between the rows of remaining corn-stalk stumps, his leather riding boots sticking into the mud with each step. He pauses to spark a match on the butt of his gun, lights a pipe taken from his pocket, and continues his regiment. The night is cold and damp. The rain has stopped, and a thin mist hangs in the tops of the tall pines. Water gathers in low-lying places in the fields, and the wind is still, even the crickets are silent. The sky is clear of clouds and filled with the twinkling lights of the stars. The moon; glowing low and bright. He keeps to his vigil well; pacing, guarding and smoking. The moon watch-ing. Fog rolls lazily out from between the dark trees and slowly moves towards the posted guards. The wind howls through the forest, and crosses the fields and fires, snaking through the wooden shacks, whistling between cracks in boards, carrying on it the sounds of their wailing and shrieking. Soon it will be time.

The wood and thatch cottage was quiet. Warm in the chill night from a fire roaring in the hearth, the smells of roasting meat and vegetables and wood smoke filling the air and nostrils. A woman with dark hair and a green dress stirs a pot over the fire, singing softly to herself as she does; the sound of her voice barely louder than the hissing and popping of the logs on the fire. Her husband sits in a chair beside the hearth, brow furrowed, sharpening the blade of a hand-ax, his dog curled up at his feet. A shotgun stands propped against the wall by the wooden door, which is bolted and barricaded with iron. In the room, a small boy lies upon a bed, turning over in his restless sleep, clutching the blankets tighter around him. The dog at his master's feet-unmoving and asleep-suddenly jerks his head upright; ears perked up, nose sniffing madly into the air. He turns his head to the door, and whines, so very softly, barely heard over the woman's singing. The man rises from his chair, ax in hand, and hushes his wife's song with a touch on her shoulder. She and he stood in silence, sharing a quick glance. She wrings her hands, and he tightens his grip on the ax. The only sound-the boy's breathing, the fire burning, the dog's sniffing. The wind outside the cottage was still, not a leaf on a branch stirred.

Suddenly in the distance: a howl. Piercing the silence like a knife of fear into their hearts. The dog rises and walks to the door, lips bared back, fangs showing, growling from deep within his chest, a line of hackles standing along his spine. The woman gasps, hands going to her mouth, she runs to her son's bedside and gathers him into her arms. She holds his head against her breast, her eyes brimming with tears. The child stirs but is silent as she moves a large woven rug on the floor, revealing a trap door. Hurriedly, breathing heavily, hands shaking, she opens it; taking a quick look at her husband. Still as stone, he stands by his dog by the door, ax tucked into his belt, shotgun in hand. She descends, the wooden steps creaking under their weight, into the musty cellar of dirt floor and stone walls. Crying, she sets her son in the darkness, wraps him tightly in his blanket, and kisses him on the forehead. *"Be strong for mommy, and be silent."* She tells him as she goes up the steps, closes the door, and locks it, concealing it under the rug once more.

The boy huddles, his eyes adjusting to the darkness; only small rows of light leaking through the spaces between the floorboards above him. Wooden shelves and bins line the walls, stuffed and packed with smoked and salted meats, drying onions and potatoes, harvested apples and pumpkins and gourds, and glass jars canned with foods of all sorts. The smell of dirt and dust and onions and straw fill his nose. The only sound seemingly, the hard beating of his own heart in his ears. Above him, he can hear the growling of the dog, the logs burning on the fire, and his mother's soft voice as she quietly recites prayers to the Gods. A gunshot fires in the distance, audible even down in the dark, and then much closer, a horrible scream.

The sound of the dog's growling grows to a crescendo, and suddenly the air was filled with all the sounds of hell itself. The sound of the wooden door splintering and crashing in, gunshots and such a primal noise from his father's throat the boy had never heard before, the yowling and whimpering of the dog becoming a wail and then stopping suddenly. The worst, a sound much louder than the others; the desperate screaming of his mother, and such sounds of ripping and wet slaughter that the boy rose to all fours and wretched. He curls up, covering his ears with his hands, as dark shadows crossed above, the light into the cellar flickering with their movements across the room. He closes his eyes tight and scarcely breathed, and waited. As soon as they had come, they were gone; taking with them the fire burning in the hearth, leaving behind only thick smoke whose scent was all the boy could smell over the blood. He did not move; he did not speak or make a sound. But he waited. And he cried.

Chapter 5

The Hero

Alexis Elizabeth Lynch

Solstice of Sorrow

There were once many people to go to for knowledge of what was not understood. But now, like most things, these people are no more. Lost to the land and its curse, and the beasts. The tales and stories told by the fireside, the myths and legends recited to memory, were of no help, for the knowledge was still not enough to answer the questions of the people. There remained but one choice, one place to go, and even the tales told are unsure if the old woman still lives, if she ever existed at all, or if she is only a tale; a manifestation of the years, brought about to be a thing of hope among all the darkness. It is said the old woman is a seer from the ancient times. As old as the woods itself; her magic the reason the powers of the burial grounds are still active. No one knows her real name though she has many. It is only those elderly in the village who have heard of her. For they learned such things from their fathers before them and so on. It is she who watches over the dead of the village, tends to the sacred site, and that her ancient crone form contains all the knowledge of the ancestors, and more importantly the beasts.

At mid-day, the people drew in from their homes and their harvesting, from their mourning and preparations for the winter that was nearly upon them, and they met for a discourse. A plan of action. What is to be done when nothing can be done? They gathered in the great hall; the large wood and stone building which served the town for numerable things- from civil issues to celebrations to the meeting of the elders, as well as burial rites, ceremonies, and preparations for the dead. And so it was decided after much discussion and outcry and woeful outbursts filled with hopelessness, that someone would be sent out of the village on a quest for the ancient seer told of in tales. In most circumstances, it was laughable to try and find something that does not exist. But the beasts had risen to stalk upon the land once again, and every soul dwelling there was powerless to confront or change it in any way.

And so she was chosen. A young woman, daughter of a renown hunter, who's other passion aside from stalking deer trails in the thick trees, was the study and history and happenings of her ancient people, their ways, their magic, and their curse. Though it could be said that she choose herself, for when the moment was upon them, not a person offered up themselves for the task. The silence and tension are palpable in the air. She rose from her seat and walked to the center of the hall, where a large fire burned in a circular pit, the air thick with smoke curling upwards along with the worry of her people. Their hopeless, haunted, desperate faces cast with shadows from the firelight, were pleading to her in the dark. The task was daunting, and even more so for it was known to be a futile act and a sacrifice of one's very life. But unwavering she stood before them and took the entire weight of her people onto her shoulders.

So she gathered her gun-belt and saddled her horse. A stocky workhorse used for plowing fields and pulling wagons; his coat the color of storm clouds, his mane and tail black as night. The sun had just risen after a night of silence. She mounted her horse and at a walk, they meandered through the dirt and deserted streets of the town. Past bolted doors, and over the wooden bridge spanning the river until at last, they were in the harvested fields. The great forest stood before her, ominous as a gaping maw, swallowing her up as she rode on into the trees. The woods were still; not even the birds had awoken to sing. The fog lay low on the ground, and the pine boughs dripped with dew.

Chapter 6

The Seer

Alexis Elizabeth Lynch

Solstice of Sorrow

(O)nward into the forest she rode until reaching the burial grounds, where she dismounted and went to kneel; eyes closed and voice soft as she spoke prayers to and asked guidance from the Gods. Her horse stood waiting calmly-for there is nothing to be feared on that hallowed ground. After, she continued on riding, farther and farther north, deeper and deeper into the forest, far beyond the familiar trails and trees where the people hunted. Every boulder and stream and rise of the valley were now unfamiliar to her. Yet still she rode on. It is mid-day, but the coniferous trees are so tall and towering and thick that the sunlight can barely penetrate through to the ground. The wind began to pick up; howling like far-off wolves through the tree branches, and on it came the smell of smoke. She reins her horse to a stop and smells into the air, and suddenly it seemed as though the wind carried on it the sound of music; drums and harp and a kind of wailing song, sung in an old language she could not understand. She sat upon her horse and waited, listening, thinking perhaps it had all been imagined. But the music continued, and she turned her horse into the wind, riding closer to the source of the sound. It was barely a whisper in her ears, an echo in the trees, but it was there.

Then ahead, at the base of a valley, smoke curled above the treetops. She dismounted and led her horse at a slow walk towards it, their feet and hooves rustling over dead leaves like dried bones. And there-in a clearing of the trees, stood a massive tree unlike all the others. It was a deciduous tree, naked of all its leaves, massive and towering and dead. From a low hanging branch, a rotting crow hung upside down from its feet from a piece of twine, its wings outstretched, spinning slowly. The branches creaked and rubbed together in the wind, sounding like the screeching of monsters. In the shadow of this behemoth dead tree, sat a cottage. It had walls of stone and its roof a blanket of moss, a weathervane perched upon its peak. Smoke rose from the stone chimney, and a window in the front of the cottage was closed over with a wooden shutter and iron paddle-lock. She stood staring in disbelief, in amazement, at the dwelling. What were the chances? If the ancient crone existed, then there was truth to all the other tales as well. The thought was like a stone in her stomach, a great weight in her heart. Surrounding the cottage was a wrought-iron fence that stood chest high, the tops brutally sharpened into jagged spikes, the entire thing covered in thick blankets of ivy vines, concealing it. She tied her horse to a tree and entered through a gate not covered by ivy and closed it behind her. She walked down the stone path leading to the front door, which was wooden and seemed to have been taken from an immense tree, its grain and color polished smooth, its edges gnarled as roots. Raising her fist to knock on the thick door, it suddenly swung open revealing a dim room. She could smell and see the fire roaring in the hearth. She stepped inside, and the door closed immediately behind her.

Eyes adjusting, she looked around. Shelves and tables were stuffed to overflowing with various plants and books, precious stones and animal bones, unknown specimens preserved in jars, and numerable other things for which she had no name, for she had never seen anything like them before. Drying herbs hung in bundles from the ceiling beams, and a large black cauldron sat upon the fire. The smoke curling upwards from its surface was the color of the moon, and the snow, and sunlight reflecting over water. And suddenly, among the clutter, there she was; at a table, hunched over, her hooked beak nose nearly touching the scroll of parchment which she read. Her skeletal hands and fingers moved as spiders, casting stones and bones onto the table, mumbling in a strange tongue the girl could not understand. And then quickly-she looked up- her eyes pale as moons, misted over and foggy, staring straight through and into her as she stood by the door. The crone lifted a hand and beckoned with a motion of her finger. Hardly daring to breathe she walked forward to stand by the table near her.

Her skin was soft and wrinkled as old leather; she had not a tooth in her mouth and her hair sheer silver that brushed the floor when she moved. Her voice sounded of dried leaves rustling across the ground, like logs on a fire crackling as they burn. *"You seek what was searched for before you, yet you do not know what it is. You are here for knowledge, for answers. I do not have the answers. The Reckoning. The end to all that is that plagues and consumes this land. Some things cannot be undone, but you already know this child. And the beasts know as well. Stare long enough into the abyss, and the abyss looks back into you. I have long had forces who oppose my readings, my rites. The old ways are dead, and I myself am nearly gone, all forgotten. The burial grounds are sacred because it is hallowed ground; the only place where they cannot tread. The beasts have great power, perhaps more so than my own. My respect for them is equal to my fear of them. We all must die sometime child. That is the way of this world and always has been. Our only escape from the daemons is to sleep, like the ancestors in their graves. "* The crone threw back her head and laughed, the sound like crows cawing madly to each other, the sound of grinding metal and stone. The wind picked up outside, sounding like ghosts all around the cottage, and the candles snuffed out, and then the fire under the cauldron quieted down to embers, and the room fell into darkness.

Alexis Elizabeth Lynch

Chapter 7

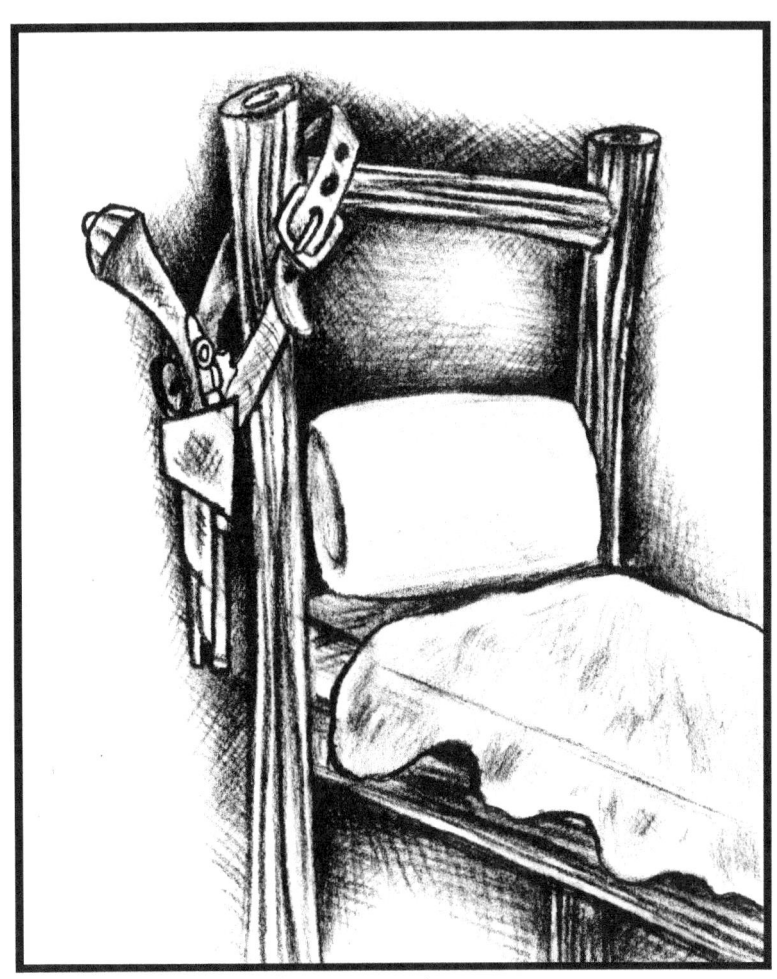

The Awakening

Alexis Elizabeth Lynch

Solstice of Sorrow

𝕿ossing and shaking in her sleep, she dreamed. Vivid images of blood trails in the snow, being lost among trees and shadows with no direction out, and an end of a night where the sun didn't rise. Then, in a flash, the stench of old blood, dusty books, wet dirt, and eyes; like large pale moons set back against a consuming dark of a pupil. With a violent scream she awoke; eyes wide with terror and face wet with tears. Damp with sweat, her skin erupts in goosebumps, the hairs along the spine and neck rising. Nights like this always happen for a reason.

Outside a storm picks up and rages. The rain beats incessantly against the locked shutters barricading the window. Gusts of wind grab them and violently shake them on their hinges. Thunder echoes loudly like the far-off explosions of dynamite, rumbling the frame of the house down to its very foundation. The dirt roads and the fields have turned to mud, beginning to collect water in the concave places. The creek and river flow and push madly against the banks with the abundance of water. The light of the stars are all but lost; the masses of cumulonimbus pregnant with water, crawling slowly like tar across the sky. The forest and trees have become white, the wind flipping the leaves over onto their bellies, shaking like wet paper from their thin stems.

Total darkness covered the entire house, and even after her eyes adjusted themselves to being awake, it was still nearly impossible to distinguish the room or the looming shapes of furniture and walls of her home. Lying amongst the blankets still tangled from a restless sleep, she slides her hand slowly between the sheets next to her, and her fingertips hit cold steel. The rifle lay beside her, out of habit. Its heavy presence; a comfort, and the only way she can fall asleep. Still laying down, she reached for a cigarette; delicately reaching into a leather pouch on her gun belt hanging from the bedpost, and pulling one out. Holding it between her lips like a kiss and striking a match on the wooden bed frame, she lit it. Drawing the rough smoke into her lungs, she exhaled with a sigh of satisfaction; the smoke covered the smell of the worms from the storm. Thousands of squirming bodies; pink flesh writhing with pain, drowning in saturated dirt and gasping for air. Mucus sticking to the soil around them in globules as they break the surface of the ground and die. Thousands of souls wandering in the rain. It was an off-putting realization, but the sickly wet smell of dead worms turned her stomach more than the smell of the pools of blood, and freshly gutted organs of man did. After an attack, the scent of old blood and intestines left in the sun hung pungently in the village for days. Smelling it was inevitable, inescapable. It had become as familiar as smelling wood-smoke from the fires, or the scent of gunpowder in the night.

Pulling her flintlock pistol out from its holster, she holds it securely between her knees and reaches determinedly towards the pouch of reloading supplies on the bedside table. Her fingers contact and meticulously pull out the tools as she needs them; the smell of leather and gunpowder and oil filling the air. Repetition leads to habit; her fingers working with familiarity in the darkness, gently pouring the gunpowder into the steel barrel of the weapon. She pauses, then pushes a heavy ball of lead wrapped in an oiled patch of cloth down into the barrel, compacting it against the powder with the ramrod. She has done this too many times, needed to do it for far more than hunting. It is a skill she would have rather not mastered. The metal of the rod clinks conspicuously against the spherical bullet and the silence; the sound itself stirring her courage in the dark. She sighs, slowly priming the flash-pan, running her finger along the jagged chunk of flint, and returns her supplies to the nightstand. She finishes the tedious work, and leans against the headboard, cocking back the hammer, the pistol held across her knees. She waits, lost in thought. She is far away from this room, somewhere else entirely. The glowing orange ember from her lit cigarette held securely in her mouth, the only light in the room.

The storm has passed, and all is still but the dripping of water outside. The wind carries on it the smell of the damp and smoldering fires surrounding the village; Soon, it will be time. The fires smell as they always have before fate brought upon them this suffering. In those days, sleepless nights and dreams filled with images of her own death didn't plague her. Before, there was not so much blood on her hands, and a man to keep her bed warm instead of a gun. Even now, there is no hope. One can always rebuild the village, re-sew the fields. But, some nightmares will always haunt her sleep. Some things cannot be undone. Lighting her cigarette again, and taking a drag, she waits patiently. It is a twisted life. She sometimes does not know if she has woken up, or if she is still asleep. How does she know what reality is? Even her dreams are filled with blood. When she awakes, she can smell it fresh on the wind outside; the only evidence or proof of the slaughter that took place while she was fighting restlessly in her sleep.

And there – loud and brash against the silence, the creak of a floorboard just beyond the barred door. Can there be no escape from this?

Alexis Elizabeth Lynch

Part 2

Springtime

of

Surrender

Alexis Elizabeth Lynch

Chapter 1

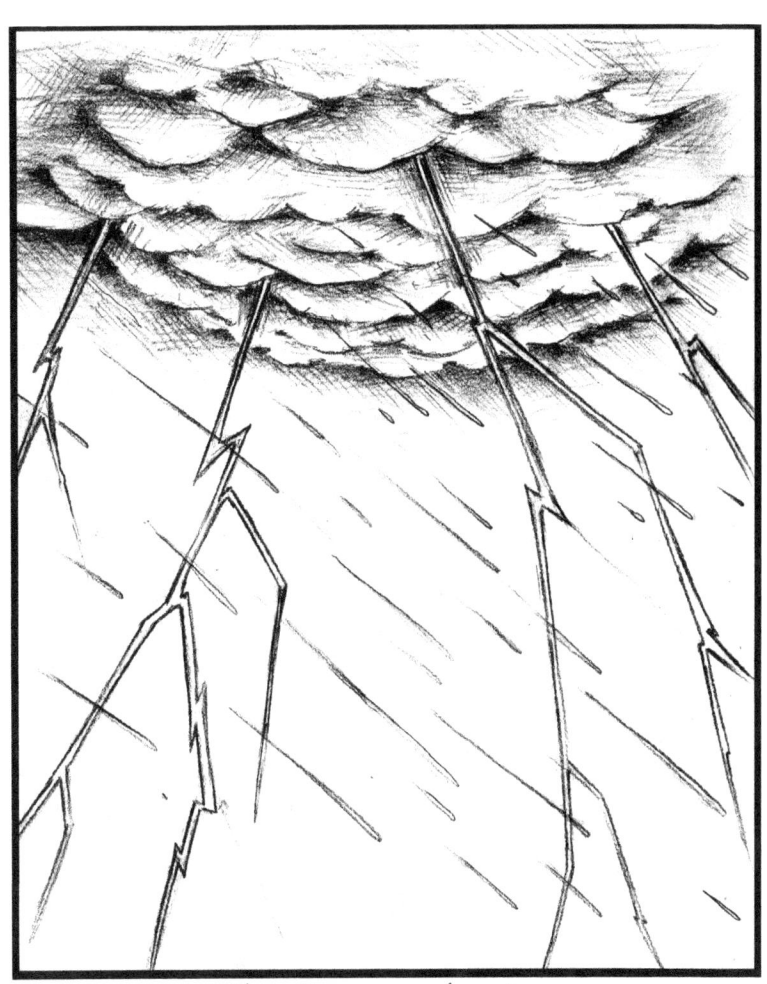

The Remembering

Alexis Elizabeth Lynch

Springtime of Surrender

It was Springtime. The snows and long nights of the Winter were in the past. It was nearing the day's end and it had not rained all the day long. Fields had been turned over, fresh seedlings planted, animals birthing their young, and trees sprouted buds which opened their fuzzy soft fresh new petals to the sunlight. It would have all been a rather pleasant time of year, a much-needed respite from the onslaught of the harsh Winter. Alas, this was not so. The Beasts still came, though now, no longer with the snows, but with the rain. Today was a good a day as any, and the villagers were tired but happily fulfilled after a productive day.

Yet, she still wished to remain asleep, and not emerge into the light. She had spent most of her day in bed. In slumber, you feel much of nothing when you try to and want to. She had yearned for sleep; her eyes were heavy with it but the dreams haunted her, and she couldn't bear it much longer. There was not much more of this life-awake or dreaming that she could bare for much more. She felt as though she had tired of her skin, and she wished to re-move it. She wished to be stone. To feel nothing. To take the long sleep and be enveloped in the comforting dark-ness. Waking up was hard to do. She felt the need to be lost in the nothingness that was sleep. It was a relief to be rid of her pain, if only for the night. It had been raining for days but finally, it had stopped. The nights were as chilled as her heart. Her sorrow always seemed to come with the rain. It seemed most at home then. She watched the rain falling outside her window and felt the cold of the wind and the cold of her heart as she began to be blanketed in a feeling of nothingness.

The nights were long and restless and her food didn't settle well, always like stones in her belly, heavy like the darkness which consumed her. The deer were bedded down for the night. And she was awake. The nightmares had not stopped. Her visions only became wilder and more frequent and more lucid. Nights were the longest and days were filled with distraction to keep her mind occupied. Things were not so bad in the hours of the day. And at night, it was the worst; These Beasts from the forest, and those inside her. Both fighting to destroy and only she standing in the middle of life and death.

She had left the village before, though, after all of it, she had not been sure if it had been a dream or reality. She did not remember her journey home. The old crone's words still echoed like a ringing in her ears, and then it all went dark. She had awoken in her bed but remembered nothing before that moment. It had left her feeling helpless and hopeless for days. Then some fellow villagers had recanted the meeting at the town hall, and stories of the excitement of their children as they followed behind her horse as she rode through the town. So then she knew it had all been real. Had it been a dream, maybe it would have given her comfort. But alas, she had nothing to provide the villagers with; No explanation, no support, no hope. So she had avoided them, remaining barricaded inside her home, or taking her night patrols alone, looking up into the night sky, imploring the moon to give her the guidance or peace she needed and longed for. She could hear the whispers of the villagers after she had returned empty-handed and heavyhearted. They were losing hope and losing faith; in her, in themselves, in the value of their own lives.

Suicide deaths increased substantially after she had returned from her journey into the forest to find the old woman seer. If there was no help to be had, some would rather take their own lives than to let the Beasts have their soul. There was no one and nothing left for her among the townspeople. She had nothing that held or kept her there, other than it was her favorite place to rest her head, and this is where she and her husband had made a life together. Now he was gone, and she could carry the memories of their love and their life together along with her wherever she went. So she had at last decided to leave again, but this time she would not return until it was finished. This time it was a one-way mission. All that stood between the beasts and the village and another thousand years of bloody hell-was she. The responsibility was overwhelming.

It seemed that everything in her life was coming to a close. This was not the end of another chapter, but the end of the story. The end of it all. The conclusion, finalization, and convergence of her entire life that has led up to this moment. What has happened has been retribution for her own poor choices in life. Call it consequences, call it karma, but whatever it may be called-she felt she was being punished and her anguish was such that she could not bear to withstand it for much longer. Her husband was killed by the beasts. At least she had no children to hide from their jaws. They had tried for years, and she turned out to be as barren as the fields outside her windows were this time of year. It had never made him love her any less; at least that's what he had always said when she'd cry about her inadequacies. But she knew. After all, what makes a woman a woman other than her body's own gift of childbirth? The only real magic left. And she had none.

And now he and his strong and tender hands, rough palms and soft fingers, and all the children they would never have; gone. Gone now like the long winter and the snows which had fallen for so long this past season. But

47

not the rain, nor the fear, nor the Beasts. That all remained. She wanted to leave, but she did not know how to bring herself to leave the people of the village even if there was a way to do it. How could life be so unbearable and hopeless, and yet worth so much? Why is a life worth fighting to preserve it? It is said that strength and love come first from within. That to find the strength to carry on and overcome obstacles, one must pull it out from within themselves. To steady the nerves and breathe deeply and calmly, and draw one's self into a focused mind. That it is the foundation upon which strength is built upon. Love also starts from within before it can be given outwardly. What if you cannot love yourself? What if you loved someone because of how they loved you, and how they made you able to love yourself? What if a person's love gave you the strength to love yourself? Nothing is ever simple it seems. What purpose is there left when all that you loved in the world, is gone? When your source of strength has left this world, why fight to stay in it?

Chapter 2

The Orchard

Alexis Elizabeth Lynch

Springtime of Surrender

In the orchard, the apple trees were nearly in full bloom, their delicate flowers of pink and white, open to the sun and the bees. It was a beautiful sight in the morning; fresh dew glistening from the petals, and the muffled vibrations of noise from the busy honeybees rubbing themselves among erect and ready stamen and pistol, traveling from flower to flower; pollinating and impregnating. The smells carried on the wind through the houses and pastures and fields, bringing thoughts of Springtime to the villager's minds and smiles to their faces. Except for hers. The smell of apple blossoms used to wander into the open windows of her house all day. Then when her husband arrived home, the scent followed him. It was on his clothes, his hands, and his mouth. Smelling and tasting of fresh apples when he kissed and held her. He worked in the orchard. It was his passion, and he was always quite fruitful. The trees made up for what she could not. The house was always full of bushels of apples and his laugh. His strong hands holding a crisp red apple out to her, her lips and teeth coming to meet its rind of flesh, breaking through it, a burst of flavor in the mouth, across the tongue, juices dripping down her chin, his mouth there to clean it off of her, and his lips smiling against hers. The scent of apples still on his hands and they'd shed their clothes and make each other's skin sweat, his hands on her hips, firmly guiding her against him. Such happy memories; turned to ash in her mouth.

It happened while he was patrolling the orchard at sundown. The shotgun he wielded not the only sort of power he possessed, but the one which would protect him from the Beasts. Or so he thought. The night was clear and crisp and still. The moon shone down through the branches of the apple trees, and the stars glistened like his eyes did when he laughed. It was autumn time, a low mist crawled across the ground between the trees, and all the evil spirits of the veil ran amok through the night. And he was out patrolling among his beloved harvest with only a mortal weapon to protect him. The firm ground and dried leaves crunched beneath his boots and the other men were strengthened by his calm demeanor and the courage he carried with him on the night patrols. She had wanted him to stay home that night. She did not want to be alone. She felt fear more than usual, and her instincts were telling her to keep him close. It was a full moon, and it affected her as profoundly, as it affected the Beasts. She thought they must have gained their power from the moon, for when it hung full in the night sky, their blood-lust and ferocity were unmatched. The likes of which had never been seen before, even after so much death already.

She had finally fallen asleep, hard as it was without him next to her in bed. She tossed and turned all night, eventually falling out of this world and into her dreams. There were images of the apple orchard and the moon. Apples with rinds of blood, fog filled with glowing eyes, and the taste of sweat, the sounds of howls, and her husband; picking an apple from a tree, and turning towards her, arm outstretched, offering it to her. She reaches out and takes it from him. He smiles. A spot of red appearing on his shirt over his heart. It grows; enlarging, soaking into his clothes, the blood spot spreading. His smile fades, his face twisting in pain, a yowling scream of hurt and fear escaping his lips like she'd never heard. She startled out of her sleep, sitting bolt upright, the screaming in the distance outside her windows continuing. She recognized the voice. Her heart caught in her throat, beating so heavily eventually it was all she could hear. Had his screaming stopped? She couldn't tell. She grabbed her flintlock pistol, stepped into her boots, threw a jacket over her night-dress and leaves the house; door left standing open, she took a horse from the stable and rode bareback and rein-less as fast as its legs could carry her, to the orchards.

Men still fired their guns. The smell of apples and gun smoke and the fires smoldering carried to her on the wind and hung thick as a fog in the air. The sound of howls echoed in the distance. Voices, people yelling, cries of pain, flickering lights as the fires were re-lit. She yelled and yelled his name, screaming until her voice was nearly broken. The fog was clearing and it was almost sunrise. And there-off between two rows of apple trees at the edge of the orchard, he lay. His clothes were soaked in crimson, a massive bite across his chest and shoulder. His breathing was slow and ragged and wet; the skin of his chest punc-tured and gaping as he struggled to pull in air. She held him in her lap as one would a child, the white fabric of her dress absorbing his blood, the patch of red upon them both, steadily growing. His breath smelled of apples and blood. His eyes no longer glistened like distant stars. His heartbeat was faint and fading. She cried and held him as he drifted away into the rising sunlight. His eyes meeting hers for the last time, a second which seemed to last an eternity. He lips spoke, *"I love you. I'm so sorry."* And he was gone. The sun rose over the treetops of the forest and illuminated an orchard soaked in blood and death, and a woman who had nothing else to lose in this world.

Alexis Elizabeth Lynch

Chapter 3

The Departing

Alexis Elizabeth Lynch

Springtime of Surrender

She packed what she needed which was very little, and wandered through her house, imprinting the good memories into her mind. She ran her fingers over the hewn wood walls and closed and locked all the shutters over the windows. It seemed as though everything here reminded her of him. His smell no longer lingered, but at times his laughter would echo through the empty rooms, or his shotgun would end up between the sheets in the bed next to her. Or she'd wear one of his old shirts, desperately searching for any scent of his skin that still clung to the fabric. That was as close as she could ever get to him unless she was dreaming. She was surrounded by sadness in her own home. She packed food and water, her maps, her guns and ammunition, food for her horse, some clothes, her tent and bedroll, his favorite hunting knife, and his leather duster coat. There was not much else she needed where she was going, and in the end, she wouldn't be able to take any of it with her.

The map she had copied out of an old book from the archives, was far more extensive and detailed than her own maps. When it came to the forest and lands north of the village, she was quite familiar with the areas and had made her own maps for hunting. She had also purchased maps of distant lands from the merchants who had traveled from the south. She enjoyed knowing how the area and its settlements were laid out in relation to each other. But this map was very old and unlike any of the ones she had seen before. Everything was called by more ancient and illegible names than what the villagers called the landmarks now. Some were even in a language she did not comprehend. The compass rose [the circular symbol upon a map dictating the primary inter-cardinal directions] inscribed upon it was more intricate and beautiful than she had ever known a human hand to create. And at its center was a full moon, the points of the directions encircling it, all effigies of tooth and claw.

It was an ancient map, which showed the forest in its entirety, green ink looming ominously over most of the parchment. To the far north were the mountains. The river that wound through their town was fed by a large lake, whose shape looked like a drop of blood upon the parchment. Old as it may be, the sacred burial ground was drawn and labeled plain as day, it's marking upon the map a circle of black stones with a red fern growing in its middle. Other things were marked as well-symbols she did not recognize, places she had never been. But also places that were familiar. She had taken her own personal hunting map, and laid it on top of this one, tracing its ancient lines onto her own map, matching it up as best she could. Some things had changed; the forest has indeed been more extensive then, covering the place where her village now lay and grew even farther into the south lands. And many years ago, a fine stone castle once stood where the village is. But time changes and seasons are harsh, and now all that remains of the castle is the stone rubble scattered along the edge of the woods. It is a long forgotten dwelling of the ancestors, the ones who brought the curse down upon them, and unto all others who would come to dwell upon these lands.

Upon this ancient map were markers along the edges of the lake to the north, indicating dwellings of some kind. She had known of gypsies that were said to live in that region, but that was years and years ago before the Beasts had returned, and now that they had, there was no way of knowing if the gypsies had even survived. They were a secretive and superstitious people, their culture remaining untouched for a thousand years. They most likely would have been run out to the mountains to the north or slaughtered. But it was an option that she had not tried yet. These native dwellers had always been the source of stories, superstitions, and various skills of divination and the occult. The lake itself was so vast, that though it was freshwater, sometimes it acted like the ocean. In times past it had been quite the hub for trading ports between the ancient stone city that stood where the village now is, and those remote outposts, encampments, and villages north that were in the forest and surrounded the base of the mountains. Now the village was the northernmost settlement in the entire region, relying on trade to the south to help sustain them and bring them the news. Since the beasts had returned, the traders and travelers from the south had stopped. Now they were truly isolated and alone in all the world.

Her horse was packed, her house was secured, and no one knew that she had been planning to leave again. She mostly kept to herself. At times, she thought they were afraid of her. After all, she had ventured into the forest alone, passed the night, and returned home alive. It had never been done before. It was best they did not know she was going there again. They could not bear any more disappointment; she had already taken all the hope they had. According to the map, it would take her nearly all day or more to reach the lake. She had never been that far north before, and after she passed through her own woods of familiarity, she did not know what to expect. Her night had been restless; she did not get much sleep. So she used the cover of darkness to make her preparations, as to not disturb the villagers, or alert them to her intentions.

It was early, just before sunrise, when she left home. She rode along the outskirts of town and took the wooden covered bridge that crossed the river beside the apple orchard, and entered the forest. This was a common route the early morning hunters would take, but now they all slept on oblivious of her passage. She reined her horse to a stop and looked back at her village. Her heart pulled in her chest, sadness tight in her throat. She had grown up here. This place was her whole life. She was looking at her home for the last time, and it hurt. She knew, in the end, she would be dead from all this, whether it be here in the village or out there among the trees of the forest, so she may as well make another attempt to bring this curse to an end. To bring the Beasts trembling to a halt on their warpath. Nudging her horse forward, they disappeared into the trees, and she did not look back.

Chapter 4

The Journey

Alexis Elizabeth Lynch

Springtime of Surrender

She rode on at a steady pace for most of the morning. These woods were familiar to her. As the day wore on, she entered unfamiliar surroundings and things went more slowly. The map was clearly marked, and she had decided to take the easiest route-one that followed the main river. She would not get lost and eventually it would take her to the lake. She could ford the other smaller streams as needed. The forest had abundant wildlife, and all the trees and wildflowers were in bloom. Even her Noriker Draft horse was in good spirits; Seemingly prancing along and whinnying joyously, as the sun broke through the trees and warmed his gun-smoke colored fur and black mane. She stopped along the riverbank to let her horse drink his fill. She fed him apples, and she chewed on dried beef leftover from her winter stores. It was unsettling how beautiful the forest was now. She had been so used to the haunted dark trees and shadow-filled fog at night that she had forgotten why she had loved to be out among the trees. In her youth, she had spent more time in the forest than in her own house. And now, she would never go back. These trees were to be her new home.

She traveled for many miles, and as she rode, the trees around her continued to get larger and taller and grew farther apart. It felt ethereal and otherworldly. She had not known that trees could grow to be so big. It was now dusk, the shadows growing, the birds returning to their nests, the frogs and crickets and fireflies emerged. The river had become wider the more northwards she traveled, and it now spanned over 200 feet wide. She found a nice place along the bank and settled in. She unpacked her horse, brushed him, and hobbled him for the night. He stood eating grass and plants

and watched her work. She made a fire, set up her

63

tent, prepared her bed, and ate. Exhaustion wore heavy upon her after the long day's ride, though there was much on her mind to keep her from sleep.

Tonight the sky is heavy with darkness. It lays on me as I try to sleep, making my body uneasy and restless. The wind carries whispers through the trees around me, and in them, I hear your voice. Crawling from my bedroll and out of my shelter on hands and knees; I look up. The moon hangs like quartz above me, from where I stand, it glows small enough to fit in my palm. A jewel I can never wear. The stars glitter like billions of shattered prisms, shaping themselves into signs I can read; a cosmological language. My fire burns small but bright, sending the shadows flickering and dancing onto the trees and into the woods around me. The night is humid with the smell of wood-smoke and skin sticky with sweat and dirt. Unable to sleep, I rummage through my gear, gathering bits of jerked beef and water, as well as tobacco, and place myself again next to the fire. Fixating on the rising smoke, I try to read the signs, but there is nothing to be seen. Man or God or Beast, we all must do what we must. I cannot keep us from our fates.

This night weighs like a stone on my chest, and so does this distance between us. Farther every day. I wish I had more on this empty night, other than a gun to cradle me. The talk of the owls echoes deeply through the trees, sounding like lost ghosts and never what they seem. Crickets chirp incessantly in the underbrush, their clicks ticking away the seconds, the minutes. A slow passing of time that cannot be ignored. The warmth of the fire warms my face like a morning sun, though; there is a chill seeping through my bones that I cannot be rid of. I long for touch and presence, be it man or God or Beast, for I am alone in all the world and these miles and minutes and nights bare much weight on my soul.

How do you find something that's been lost for hundreds or thousands of years? How do you resurrect something from beyond the veil of the dead? The laws of the universe have been the same since before the beginning, and they will continue on in the same stringent manner, until all of our world is so far gone, faded into the past, it will be as though none of it had ever existed in the first place. But even then I suppose the Beasts would remain, since they were here long before the village, maybe long before us. These attempts, logically all seem to be in vain. How does one make the raindrops not fall? How do you command the moon to not rise for a night? Must all things so necessary for the greater good, be so utterly difficult? Do the Fates see it fit to mock our struggle? Do they enjoy our suffering, and turbulence, and inability to stop that which haunts us?

What is it that separates a woman scorned, from the Beasts? Both seek to destroy. Wolves are not evil-they kill to eat, not for pleasure. The Beasts, as far as any of them could tell, did not eat unless they sufficed with feeding upon the darkness or the rain. Perhaps upon something more palpable, like the endless sorrow of the people in the village. It was not in short supply. So indeed a woman scorned, a desperate woman with nothing left to live for, is indeed a dangerous creature. Much like the beasts. Not killing to eat. Killing for the desire of it. How contradictory a place the world is.

Alexis Elizabeth Lynch

Chapter 5

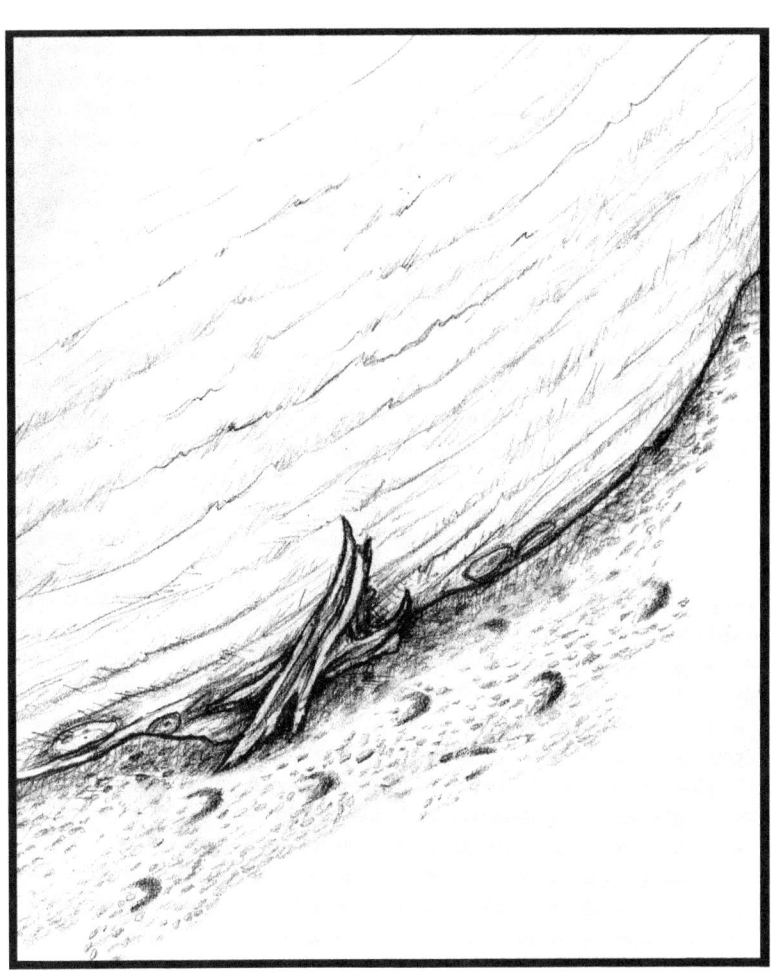

The Lake

Alexis Elizabeth Lynch

Springtime of Surrender

The sun rose over the massive treetops and with it the birds. She awoke, packed up camp in the light of the morning sun, and she continued north towards the lake. She could smell the water before she could see it. At last, up ahead, the light reflecting off of the water's surface broke through the trees. She pulled her horse to a stop at the edge of the tree line and looked across the massive lake. It took the breath from her lungs. It was even larger than she had expected, and even with putting her hand up to shield her eyes from the sun, she could not see the far edge of the lake. To the north and half-covered in clouds towered the mountains. They stood sharp and ominous and nearly consumed the entire sky beyond. Thick grown trees surrounded the lake, its shore strewn with smooth dark stones. The water nearly clear-the stones could be seen on the bottom, and the water of the lake was black where it grew deep. Her horse drank from the lapping shore while she stared in awe. She felt small in this world. How was her life or her village even significant when compared to those mountains or this lake?

The wind picked up slightly and blew from the north, and she caught the scent of wood smoke. Was this real? Did she imagine it? She turned to the north, urging her horse to a slow walk along the shore, strong legs pushing down into the sand and smooth rock, the tide lapping at his large hooves. She scanned the forest. And there! Was that smoke curling above the treetops? She watched for awhile, and the smoke continued, and again she could smell it. It was daytime, mid-afternoon, but she was nearly to the mountains. The cold slid off their steep faces and down into the valley, making the springtime weather a bit chilly so near to the water, despite the sunlight. She refilled her water pouches and entered the forest again from the northern side of the lake, making her way towards the smoke. She referenced her map for safe places to cross the tributaries stretching out around the lake. She glanced up; the markings upon the map for the gypsy dwellings along the lake geographically matched the direction the smoke was coming from. Her heart skipped a beat and her stomach flipped. How is it possible anyone could have survived the onslaught of the Beasts, especially so deep in the forest, and so close to the mountains where the beasts were thought to have come from?

The winter was over, and that was the season the Beasts loved the most. The crisp air put a fire in their blood and the snow was the best for concealing their movements. The springtime was upon them now and the hunting had slowed but not stopped. In the cold times of the year, they left no tracks, moved with the wind and moon, and a had thick layer of fur to warm them. Now the cold times had at last passed, and they had shed most of their fur. Their massive bodies looked nearly skeletal; sharp bones protruding, the skin stretched tight over their ribs, the large red eyes sunk even farther into their skulls. They were terrifying to behold.

They were said to not be much like wolves at all. Firstly, they were much too big to be mere wolves. More like the Dire-wolves of ancient times. But in ancient times, and farther back than that, it was said that they were daemons who only took the form of the monstrous Beasts. It was unknown if they slept. One only figured they hid from the sun, deep in the dark bowels of the mountain. Much was unknown. But the Beasts knew when the moon rose, and where the village lay, and that was enough. The crisp wind picked up and blew from the south. On it was carried her smell and that of her horse. The wind wound its way through the trees and to the north. Snaking its way between the rocks and slithering its way into the fissures. Down deeper and deeper under the mountain it blew. In the darkness, they smelled the scent. And unbeknownst to the rest of the world-the Beasts stirred.

Alexis Elizabeth Lynch

Chapter 6

The Gypsies

Alexis Elizabeth Lynch

Springtime of Surrender

She traveled northward through the forest following her nose to the source of the smoke. The trees were thicker here, the ground steadily becoming rockier, giant boulders protruding from the ground, massive outcroppings of rock which she wove around and between. It was disconcerting, and after awhile she felt as though she was no longer heading north. At last, she emerged from the labyrinth of rock into an area which opened up. The ground was smooth, and the trees encircled the space. And there, at its center, was a campfire, still burning, its smoke curling upwards into the open sky. She looked around, but there was nothing else to behold, other than the campfire. No tracks of any kind. No noise. No signs of life. Warily, she dismounted and walked her horse towards the fire. She stopped next to it and looked up to find the sun and tell which direction she was heading. She could not find it, and she pondered. She checked her map-for she could not tell where she was.

Focused on her thoughts, the sound of music slowly broke its way through her concentration, and she recognized it as the music which had led her to the Seer in the forest in the south those many moons ago. She looked up, and suddenly she was surrounded by what seemed to be a small village of gypsies. Wooden caravans with arched roofs encircled the area. Clothes hanging to dry, dogs asleep in the sun, women cooking over fires, children running and playing among the trees, men chopping firewood or tending livestock, young girls milking goats. The sound of bells, laughter, and music. The smell of food and incense and animals. And a group of elderly women sitting around the fire by which she stood. She stood in disbelief. Was she hallucinating? Was this real? She reached forward to touch the flames and felt the sharp heat brush her fingers in pain. One of the elderly women laughed and shook her head, motioning to an empty space upon the ground beside her.

She sat with them, leaving her horse to be taken away by a group of children, who fed him apples and oats, braided his hair, and began painting ancient symbols upon his body in red ochre. She was oblivious to this, as she sat and stared at the ancient women seated in the circle around the fire with her. It seemed as though she had forgotten how to speak, or if she had ever even had a voice at all. She could not find the words, and she did not think that her mouth would have been able to speak them. In turns, the three elderly crones spoke, each picking up where one left off. A seamless flow of words and voices intermingled until they seemed like one. Suddenly, nothing else existed. Only them, around the campfire, and the words. Their voices seemed to speak aloud, and inside her head.

"We have been watching you. Since you were born, and long before. It has been known that this meeting would come to pass. We know you search for answers. About the curse. The Beasts. Your Husband's death. The children you don't have. There are many questions, so many, and yet we do not have all that which you seek. And this you already know. The Beasts are not wolves. Nor are they ghosts, or what you know as daemons. They are spirits bound by old magic. Much like you are bound by your grief. There is no escape. No end to either. They will come, be assured, as the moon comes into the dark sky each night. As the snows fall in winter, and the rains in spring, they will come. Some things cannot be broken. Much unlike the will to live. All dies eventually. Death is the only guarantee we all have. That and the passing of time, the changing of the seasons, the rising of the moon. These

spirits are bound to the mountain, and from there they can never leave. Your people could move their homes, travel to distant lands; and yes, they would be beyond the reach of the Beast's attacks. But they would carry with them the sorrow and nightmares in their heads and in their hearts, all their lives long. There can be no escape. We have told you this before; brought you to our cabin dwelling in the forest to the south, and spoke the words you had traveled so far to hear. Yet it was not what you wanted; you received no answers, so now you have returned. As was foretold. You yourself foresee that this will be your final attempt. Your last battle for freedom and release. There are only two moons, and one sun left for you now. Your journey is almost over."

"Hatred cannot kill them. Nor fear. Nor anger. They thrive on this energy. Devouring it as they do the flesh. To harm a spirit, you must become like the spirit; a sense of nothingness. You must move beyond your emotions and body and this physical realm, and exist only as energy. To defeat them you must let go. They will eat your flesh and blood. They will feed upon your mind and emotions, but they cannot destroy the force that binds us all to this life. They know you are here, but they cannot get to you until the moon rises. You will be safe here; this ground upon which we sit was once a burial ground for a people much older than even your ancients. So long ago that there is nothing left but the bones of their dead, which whisper to us, but we do not know their names. But we know the names of the Beasts. Your ancestors knew them as well. Breaking the rules of magic to learn their true name, using it to control and posses the beasts and make them devour their enemies. And now that is what the Beasts do to you. Retribution. How could you use the true name of another creature, when you do not know your own? You can't. You

77

do not have the power. You don't even have the power to control your own life. Not the power to save your husband. Not the power of being with-child. There is much for you to learn and there is no more time for you here. The burial grounds are the only sacred places left. There is nowhere else to hide in this lifetime. You much let go of everything if you are to gain anything. There must be an end before there can be a beginning. Sleep now, and when the sun rises your final journey will truly begin."

She felt herself fall into a deep sleep; the warmth of the fire blanketing her body. All was silent, and for the first time in years, she did not dream. Somewhere down inside her mind, she could hear the voices of the crones speaking to her. The same phrases over and over, in ancient languages she did not understand. They all spoke at once, their voices one, and she knew they spoke the true name of the Beasts.

"Sanctus Luna Lupus Autem Sanguinem Somina."

Chapter 7

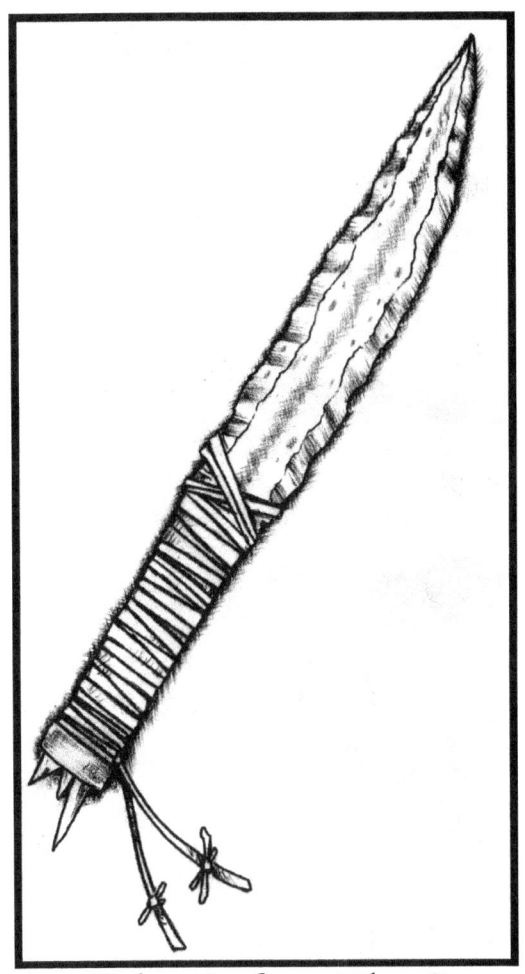

The Calm Before The Storm

Alexis Elizabeth Lynch

She awoke upon the ground, sunlight streaming down onto her face. She roused from her dreamless sleep and once again the clearing was empty of any trace that the gypsies had been there. Except for the fire pit. It no longer burned, but when she placed her hand upon a charred log, it was still warm to the touch. Then she noticed her hand and arm were painted a deep earthy red-and so was the other. She stood and looked at herself. All of her clothes had been removed except for her boots, and she now wore a loincloth, and a dark breastplate; warrior-like in design. She wrapped her knuckles against the hard plate of armor over her torso, and it sounded like a hollow tree does when the ear is upon it. Anywhere that her skin showed had been entirely painted over with red ochre. It stained her skin, hardened it, and made her feel strong. As did her new armor. Or was it magic that made her feel this way? Or was it her newfound courage to face the day? Her horse, in turn, stood patiently waiting. She stared at him in wonder. From the tips of his ears down to the bottom of his hooves, except for his braided mane and tail, he had been painted in the same style as she. He no longer looked like a horse. He was something more ancient and mystical and powerful. Her saddle was gone, but the reigns remained. Her food and water had been refilled, and her bag repacked. She sat in thought next to the smoking embers of the fire and sharpened her knife.

The sadness in her heart was paramount. Her sorrow was enough to kill her. Her misery was her own, her wretched hatred for herself and the world, and everything in it was hers to live with. The only thing keeping her alive was that the village depended upon her. Sometimes at night the rain and thunderstorms would roll in across the dark sky, and lightning would break like glass down to the ground. She'd stand out in the midst of it, tears hidden in the falling droplets of water. Wishing the lightning would strike down upon her and eat her alive. Or that the Beasts would smell her wet skin, and electrify her with their sharp teeth. But all to no avail. To take her own life would be easy. End the hurt, the pain, and the nightmares. Fall warmly into the deep sleep and be rid of this life which plagues her while she breathes awake and sleeping. She ran her finger along the edge of the blade and admired its deadly beauty. It would be quick, a bit bloody, and then the sleep. Peaceful. Wondrous. And to be reunited with the most precious thing she had ever lost. The one thing which took all of her that was broken and incomplete, and gave her wholeness and peace and contentedness in this Gods forsaken life. He was her light amidst the darkness, and now that he was gone; all that remained was the blackness of her heart.

She did not fear death. Dying would be assuredly painful unless the Fates would finally smile upon her and let her die in her sleep. But she knew she would not have it so easy. Things were never easy. So at the end of her own life, she imagined her last moments, seconds, breaths, would be painful ones. There was no getting around that, especially with how involved she had become. A hero of the people and yet she had saved them from nothing. She could not rescue them from something that could not be defeated or overcome. In the end, she would face the threat alone and would not survive the ordeal. When she was younger, she had feared death, but in youth, it is normal to fear that which is not understood. So, after all these years, after all of the destruction that has surrounded them since the first Winter of the Beasts' return, she no longer feared death. Or dying. It was a normal part of life. Without death-life would have no value. So, come as it may, she was ready as she'd ever been.

Though she was afraid of being <u>alone</u>. Death truly was the one thing you do by yourself. You can't take anyone with you. It's a journey one must take on their own. Completely. She did fear that. The black nothing. She did not fear the Beasts, nor the pain, but the fact that she would die alone. Her husband already taken by the Beasts; he would not be there to comfort her, to reassure her. To hold her hand and tell her that he would not leave her, that he would stay and watch over her as she left this world and descended into the next one. She would not die with fear in her heart, knowing he was there, and she was not alone, and that he loved her. But he was already gone, and she was alone. And she would be in the end as well, and the thought filled her with fear.

She had never minded the blood. But after so much of it for so long, it became tiring. Enough was enough. She had hunted game all her life, but now she was the one being pursued. And she was nearly done with being prey. She shouldered her pack and put her husband's hunting knife into its sheath on the belt around her waist. She whistled. Her horse let out a whinny and came to her from where he had been grazing. She grabbed a fist-full of his jet-black mane and mounted his back in one smooth motion. With her face as hard as carved stone, and her heartbeat slow and steady as a war drum, she rode into the forest heading south.

Alexis Elizabeth Lynch

Chapter 8

The Battle Within

Alexis Elizabeth Lynch

Springtime of Surrender

Steadily the day wore on and the land around her, at last, began to look familiar. The massive rain clouds had followed her south at a slow crawl all day, and now they seemed nearly upon her. At times she could hear the distant thunder in the mountains. It was almost dusk, the air was full of electricity, and the leaves on the trees flipped over in the wind, showing their bellies. The rain would be there soon, and so would the Beasts. As they traveled, they left their scent with every step her horse' hooves pressed into the dirt, with every plant they brushed against. Her trail would not be hard for the beasts to follow. The gypsies were right about one thing; tonight's moon would probably be the last she'd ever see. She was still some miles from her village's burial ground, and she nudged her horse onward, picking up the pace, and felt the hairs on her neck stand on end. Her journey from the encampment had seemed to take an eternity, she lost in her own thoughts, reflecting upon her existence. Now that she was nearly to where she needed to be, it seemed as though there was no more time left. The sky continuously darkened and the wind picked up, and she felt the first cold droplets of rain upon her shoulders and back and arms.

Then in the distance-she heard the howling. She had listened to the wolf packs that wandered the forest, crying out to each other before. It was their home more so than it was hers. Their voices were powerful and beautiful and she respected and admired them as fellow hunters. But these howls were not the wolves. The sound was something like an imitation; something that was not a wolf was attempting to howl like one. She had always been able to hear the difference. She herself had been the first to hear the sound of the Beasts when she was out hunting in the forest at dusk. She was alone, and this was before the attacks had begun. No one had believed her. It was as though the Beasts were only assuming the appearance of the wolf, to appear as something that was already recognized by the village. Something they were already afraid of. And the Spirits had indeed succeeded. Their portrayal of the Beasts as wolves was utterly terrifying. Fear began to creep into her heart as she heard the howling again, echoing through the trees, this time much closer. The rain increased and the sun was nearly set below the horizon, and her horse rose on in a gallop towards the Burial Ground. What if she could not die? What if she was fated like the Prometheus to be eaten alive over and over again for all eternity? For courage and focus, in her mind she repeated the true name of the Beasts over and over, pushing away her doubts and fears. To know the name is to know the thing. To know a true name is to have power over it.

The rain began to pour and lightning struck overhead, igniting the treetops into a blaze of hell-fire as she urged her horse through the forest. Faster and harder he ran, his breathing heavy, his booming footsteps upon the ground nearly as loud as the thunder which rolled all around them and shook the earth. The red ochre upon her skin darkened with the drops of water, mixing with her sweat, making it seem as though it were raining blood, and she was covered with a thick layer of it. Suddenly the trees surrounding them erupted with howls and shrieks, coming from all sides, the sounds nearly deafening. The massive dark shapes of the Beasts moved effortlessly through the trees around her. Skirting in and out of her vision as soon as she looked towards them, fleeting like shadows in the corners of her eyes. They were nearly triple the size of her own stocky horse, but unlike him they made no sound as they ran with her, alongside her, following behind and crossing the path before her. She knew these woods, more familiar than the walls of her home, and some distance ahead lay the Burial Ground. She ran her horse at such a fast, hard pace she was sure it would kill him soon if they continued on in this manner for much more.

The forest was nearly pitch black now; the trees only looming shapes and the path un-illuminated. The moon was full but hung concealed behind the monstrous storm clouds. Her heart was pounding, and she knew the beasts could smell her blood, and again the monsters shrieked and wailed around her, her horse whinnying in fear. Ahead the trees opened up, and she could see the faint shapes of the boulders that made up the wall surrounding the Burial Ground. The beasts encircled them closer, her horse's eyes wide with fear as they moved in and nipped at his running legs and sweaty flank. There would be no stopping the horse now. He had become dangerous; driven by fear and unresponsive to the reigns or her voice.

A Beast ran alongside them, its bones jutting, tongue lolling from the side of its open mouth, teeth as large as daggers, curved back, and white as the moon. Its eyes glowed red as she looked at the creature, and it bit into her horse's flank. Her horse faltered and crashed to the ground, throwing her off of him some distance away. The breath was taken from her lungs, and she could not breathe or move from the startling pain of the sudden impact. Her horse was in shock and struggled to get up onto its feet; a giant chunk of flesh missing from its hindquarters. The wound was down to the bone; giant teeth marks, deep enough and so sudden, that it had not yet begun to bleed. The Beasts surrounded him and swarmed upon him. Ripping and tearing off his fur and flesh, taking mouthfuls of his body, the horse screaming in terror as they ate him alive. The sounds of slaughter and bones crunching were audible over the rain and thunder. She watched her horse die for what seemed like an eternity. She regained her breath and felt nauseous. She pushed herself to her hands and knees, her stomach turned, and she retched. She looked up and was only yards from the stone wall of the Burial Ground. Turning her back on the scene of her dying horse, she crawled across the blood and mud and moss-covered ground, edging her way towards the stone wall of the sacred grounds. She was nearly there.

A dark shadow covered her and her heart nearly stopped beating. She could feel hot breath on her back and smell blood and rancid meat and the mint of the pines in the warm mist of air that surrounded her. She rolled over onto her back and found herself staring into the large eyes of one of the Beasts, which stood over her. Her faithful horse's blood covered its teeth and snout and muzzle; it dripped down onto her chest and face, and it was still warm. She was held paralyzed, overwhelmed by its existence. So all the stories were indeed real. She stared back into the eyes of the Beast. Its large eyes reflected no light. They seemed to be an infinite darkness of unfathomable depth. And suddenly she was looking into the eyes of her Husband, which did not belong to this fiendish creature, this abomination. What illusions of torture these beasts could bring to the forefront of the mind. How they know what hurts the most, and wherein to slide their blade of cruelty. She was cursed like all the rest, and she would die here in the dark woods, mind and heart and body and soul all broken and screaming in pain. Her tears mixed with the rain upon her skin, and she wished to sleep.

Chapter 9

The Burial Ground

Alexis Elizabeth Lynch

Springtime of Surrender

The Beast bent its neck and lowered its massive thick head down to her body. It opened its gaping maw and scooped her up in its mouth; sharp teeth piercing her entire torso and back, abdomen and shoulders. Its bite was huge and powerful; blades for teeth sliding into her soft flesh, meeting no resistance and scraping against her bones and through them. She screamed beyond anything she ever had been capable of, howling and crying in agony until her voice broke and she could not make a sound at all. Her blood ran across the Beast's tongue and between its teeth, dripping into a dark pool beneath her on the ground. Her mind flashed in and out of consciousness, the night sky and stars fading and refocusing. The Beast growled low in its chest, much like the sound of a cat purring. The pain was more than she could bear, and she felt like letting herself fall into the deep sleep that pulled upon her. There was not much more of her left. The Beast's saliva oozed across her skin with her blood, and with it, she could feel her life force leaving her body.

Her horse had finally died. The Beasts had consumed it entirely, bones and all, leaving nothing but a pool of blood upon the ground. The others licked their jowls and encircled the one who held her in a quandary, moving slowly like large cats on the hunt. Their deep-chest growling in unison was much like the thunder which continued. Their eyes glowed red in the darkness, they made no sound as they moved, and the rain continued to fall. A torrential downpour, relentless. Deep inside her, the names of the Beasts rose within. The sounds of their names echoed like a song or enchantment, and awakened her courage in the darkness she was consumed with. The names continued inside her, growing louder and more pronounced all the time and she roused from her nearly comatose state, opened her eyes, and looked up. The rain clouds crawled by and the moon shone down upon them. Her heart beat vigorously, as she pulled her Husband's large knife from her belt sheath. It glinted in the moonlight as she whispered the name of the Beast, and with all the energy she could muster, in one swift motion, stabbed it deep to the hilt into the neck of the Beast which held her. Its warm blood spurted from the puncture in its throat and poured over her hand and arm. It was thick and warm and black, slow moving like molasses and smelled of metal. The Beast yowled in pain and opened its jaws, dropping her to the ground, the knife still held in her tight grip as it pulled from the wound. She lay ragged in the dirt, staring into the night sky. The rain had slowed and nearly stopped. The clouds were moving away towards the mountains. She was in disbelief. Had she harmed it? It had never been done before. Was that blood, or only evil seeping from its wound?

Her time was nearly at an end; she had lost a significant amount of blood. She dragged herself piteously but with determination towards the Burial Ground, whose stone wall was almost close enough for her to reach out and touch. The Beasts watched her as she crawled across the ground, foot by foot, and they followed. The giant beast dripped black blood from its neck wound, and step by step, its large paws pushed into the muddy path upon which her limp body crawled. They waited, watching. They raised their ghost-like forms up towards the moon, and they howled and shrieked and yowled and screamed into the night sky. Their sounds filled her more than the sound of her own feint heartbeat; louder than her thoughts which screamed to her of pain and the surrender of the will to continue on.

Springtime of Surrender

She summoned the last of her willpower and crawled between the entrance stone of the Burial Ground. The Beasts paced just beyond the boundary. Back and forth, back and forth, their eyes never leaving her broken form. The rain had stopped and mist hung over the ground. As she crawled a stream of her blood trailed along the mossy ground behind her. In the moonlight, the Burial Grounds were illuminated entirely. The Beasts appeared even more ghost-like in the moonlight and their growling began again. They circled, following the outside of the stone wall, pacing relentlessly. In her blood trail, small sprouts pushed up from the dirt and moss. They were tiny curled tendrils, deep red in color, nearly the same color as her blood. They grew, uncurling, their leaves unfurling from the long stems, now as bright a red as the Beasts' eyes. The red ferns filled the river behind her that was her blood, growing tall and full, hovering above the mist which crawled across the burial sites. They grew up nearly as fast as her blood could soak into the ground.

The Beasts did not react well to this; their agitation and their bodies grew in size. They towered nearly as big as trees, eyes small blood moons, fangs of swords, bodies spectral and skeletal. They began growling and howling and snarling, snapping their jaws and biting at one another. All the time watching her. They could not enter the Burial Grounds. The land was sacred; protected by old magic even more powerful and ancient than the Beasts. But she could not stay there forever, and they had all of eternity of which to wait for her. She was entirely alone, and her death was not far off, even if the Beasts did not catch her.

She was nearly there now; she had crawled to her Husband's burial site. She collapsed on the ground in front of his headstone, thinking about how his bones lie in the dirt beneath her. Soon, they would be together again. The thought filled her with happiness she had not felt in a long time, and she cried despite not being able to feel anything else. She rolled over onto her back and stared into the night sky. The moon hung bright and full, illuminating the forest, the Burial Grounds, and the red ferns which grew all around her in the blood and nearly covered her body entirely. She gazed upwards. The edge of the galaxy was visible in the black expanse of sky; millions of stars burning in a million other worlds, and she glimpsed how insignificant her existence in this lifetime was. She still held her Husband's hunting knife, and only felt a slight pressure when she pulled it deeply across her own throat. And at last, she slept.

Chapter 10

The End

Alexis Elizabeth Lynch

Springtime of Surrender

Lightning cracked across the night sky, and thunderstorms shook the house down to its foundation. She started violently from her sleep in total darkness. Reaching between the sheets next to her, her fingertips touched something soft and warm. She screamed and clamored from her bed, hitting the wooden nightstand, unknown objects crashing to the floor around her bare feet. She cursed, fumbling for matches and the candelabra. Her hands shook as the match ignited. Wavering, she lit the candle, its soft glow illuminating the wrecked nightstand, the edge of her bed, her blanket crumpled in a pile upon the floor in her haste. She held up the candle, throwing light across her bed.

There lay someone beneath a blanket, facing away from her. They breathed deeply and rolled over to face her. Her heart caught in her throat, and her pain welled up in her chest, only finding its release through the tears running down her face. Her Husband opened his eyes slowly and stretched like a cat waking, and smiled at her, running a hand through his hair messy from sleep. He noted her distress and sat up, holding his arms out towards her. She sat down the candle upon its stand and rushed into bed, into his arms. His scent overwhelmed her, his heartbeat pounding in his chest against her cheek. He pulled her tight against him, stroking her hair, pulling the blankets around her. She cried as heavy as a child and shook like a leaf. He whispered to her, *"Darling, its okay. It was only a bad dream. I'm here."*

From another room, the sound of their baby crying echoed through the open door. In the distance, far into the mountains, a wolf howled. But she did not hear it.

Alexis Elizabeth Lynch

About the Author

Alexis Elizabeth Lynch lives at Mt Horb Farm in Ohio, and in college, she studied creative writing, human anatomy, and forestry. Alexis writes in many genres and styles including; poetry, travel journaling, screenplays, fantasy, children's short stories, non-fiction essays, and horror. She has been a guest blogger at ohiothoughtsblog.blogspot.com and has had poetry published in anthologies as well as the Columbus Dispatch. She has been the writer for Nikkso Productions since 2011, and is known for the story and screenplay of the horror film *"Tabbott's Traveling Carnivale of Terrors.".* *"Solstice of Sorrow"* is her first published novel. She is a beekeeper, a butcher, a lucid dreamer, and loves to travel with her family. She has no biological children of her own, but she does have a Goddaughter and a very long dachshund. She writes with ink and quill, and her personal library contains an estimated 3,000 books. Her favorites are Frankenstein by Mary Shelley, the Harry Potter series by JK Rowling, and the Song Of Ice And Fire series by George R.R. Martin, as well as the writings of Edgar Allan Poe & Trent Reznor.

Author Contact:

Email: WriterAEL@yahoo.com

Instagram: @alexiselizabeth_aella

Facebook: Facebook.com/WriterAELLA

Youtube: http://www.youtube.com/artsyael_

Family Blog: Ohiothoughtsblog.blogspot.com

About the Illustrators

Illustrations: Kevin Edwards

Kevin has been a tattoo artist for 16 years, specializing in macabre designs. Horror and Science-Fiction are a huge inspiration for his passion for creating art, and he has the professional skills to work with a variety of mediums and materials including canvas, paper, and skin. His favorite part of the work is seeing the ideas manifest into real life, and being able to touch the art that started as only an idea. He has done set design work for both films and live theatre performances. Other recent work includes the visual design and effects makeup of haunted houses. In his free time, he enjoys going to concerts and horror conventions, collecting horror VHS tapes, bones, and dead specimens in jars. He currently lives with his wife Crystal, daughters Sadie Mae and Leah Kennedy, and his cat Bacon.

Instagram: @ blackmoth7g

Email: deathshead7g@gmail.com

About the Illustrators

Map & Layout: Thomas S. Nicol

Thomas is the owner of Nikkso Productions, where he films and directs feature-length movies. His most favorite genre is Horror, and his up and coming film is *"Tabbott's Traveling Carnivale of Terrors"*. He spends his time with various skills and hobbies: photography, film editing, painting, composing and playing music, reading comic books, and performing feats of science and engineering. He lives in Marysville Ohio with his Son and Fiancé.

NikksoProductions.com

Instagram: @thomas_nicol_nikksproductions

Facebook: Facebook.com/NikksoProductions

Author Afterward:

I would like to thank Kevin and Thomas for all the hard work and late nights they endured for this book.

Kevin's illustrations gave life to my words in a way I never imagined possible. He exceeded expectations, and I am forever grateful. I am especially relieved he put up with me throughout the book process, as well as when I'm sitting in his tattoo chair. He did most of the art for this book while juggling the needs and shenanigans of a free-range baby, which I also find very impressive.

Thomas designed the map, and what a map it is! It took lots of research, tedious hours of drawing trees, and me always looking over his shoulder while he worked. Thomas has put up with a lot; not only while putting the book together, but while I was writing bits and pieces on again and off again for Part 2 in 2016. Sometimes as a writer, you have to travel deep into yourself or places far into the beyond, and it can be rough on those around you. I'm not the easiest person to live with or love, but he does both very well, and he is patient. I love him to the Moon and back.

I appreciate the proofreading work my Mom and Adam did for me, although it was tedious. I cracked the whip for the work, and they did it without question. (They had no idea I was publishing this book). They always catch things I miss after being submerged in the same story for weeks on end. As well, they offer creative anecdotes and feedback that gives me the fuel to carry onward. It's been a rough time for me, for quite a few years (this year was also a train wreck), and both of them have been unwavering in their love, support, and understanding. They put up with a lot, and it has certainly not gone unnoticed.

My family in general; our "inner circle," our friends, in-laws and out-laws, have done nothing but support and encourage me in my endeavors. It's lovely to have such a great support system, and I am eternally indebted. I especially want to thank my brother and his wife for making me the Godmother of their daughter. I was full of pain and very bitter for a long time about children. But having the little Goddaughter squid in my life, has helped me begin to heal and to come to terms with my own inabilities.

A Note On Pain:

All emotions, people, events, and daemons written here within, may metaphysically represent or resemble situations, relationships, and trauma experienced in your life. This was intended.

My Dad once told me, "It has to hurt so it can heal. That's how you know it's working." I agree, although the pain sometimes can be enough to kill you. It is also said, "What doesn't kill you makes you stronger" and that's just a bunch of bullshit. Just because something doesn't kill you, doesn't mean that it didn't break you. Sometimes, being broken is worse than being dead. We are told, "Everything in life happens for a reason." And sometimes you spend so much time searching for reasons, that you forget to take the time to focus on what hurt you and how. Sometimes there is no reason; never an answer that can logically quantify why it happened to you. That sucks, but that's life. We get so distracted by why and what, that we forget to heal. We don't make the time. Wounds fester. Some scars never fade. Some say "Time heals all wounds," and I don't think that's accurate. Some things can't be healed; time only makes it not hurt so badly. There are times where feeling nothing is a relief and much-welcomed. Better to learn to block it out and have control over your emotions than to have feelings or to feel pain. But this only takes the broken pieces and breaks them down more. The smaller the fragments of your being, the harder and longer a road it is to heal yourself back together.

We all have our own monsters inside, our own daemons we have to defeat, our personal trauma and obstacles and hardships. May you overcome yours or learn to live with it. Or at the very least channel your pain into healing outlets. Like your work, hobbies or passions. Or by writing a book.

Notes: